This edition published by Parragon in 2013

Parragon
Queen Street House
4 Queen Street
Bath BA1 1HE
www.parragon.com

Copyright © Parragon Books Ltd 2013

All rights reserved. No part of this publication may
be reproduced, stored in a retrieval system, or
transmitted, in any form or by any means,
electronic, mechanical, photocopying, recording
or otherwise, without the prior permission of
the copyright holder.

ISBN 978-1-84934-372-5

Printed in China

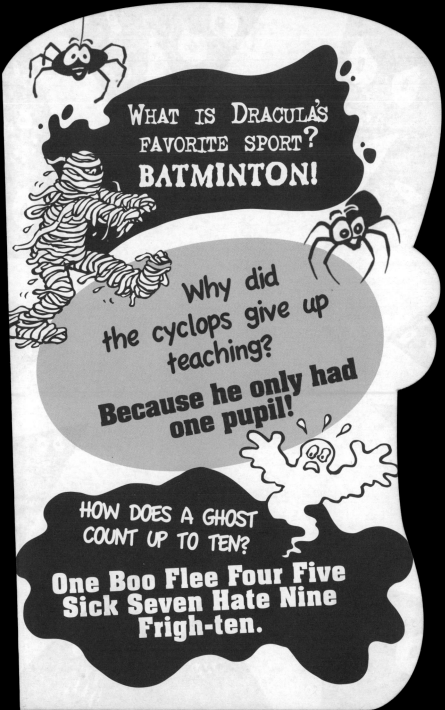

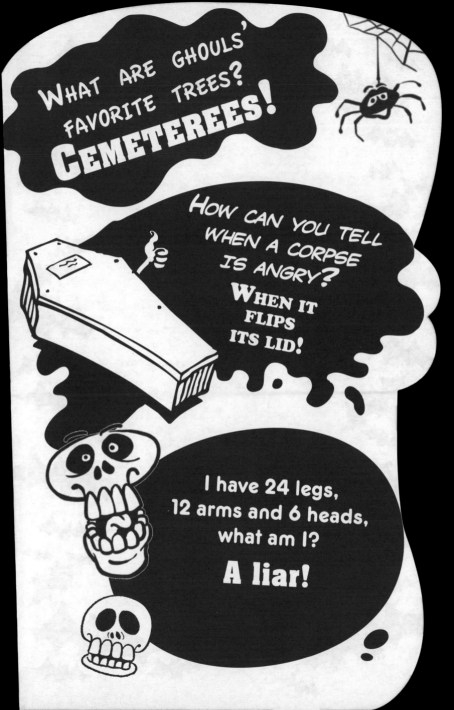

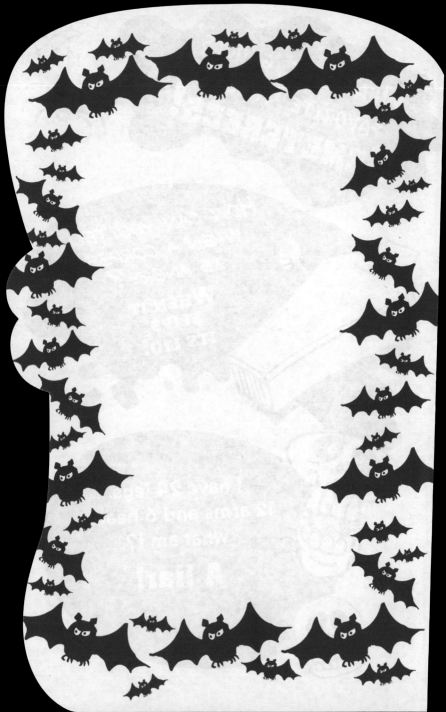

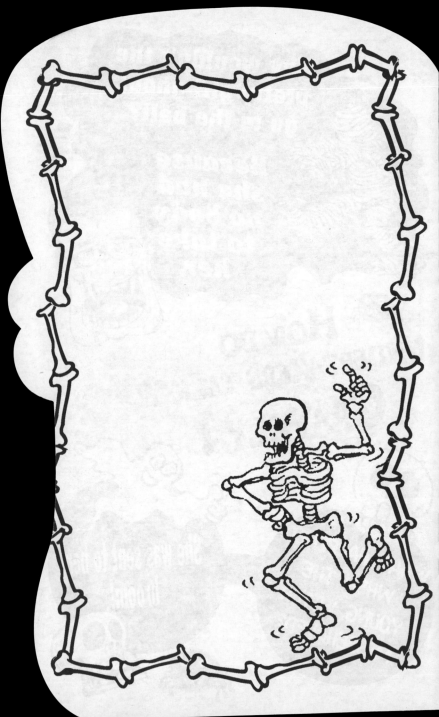

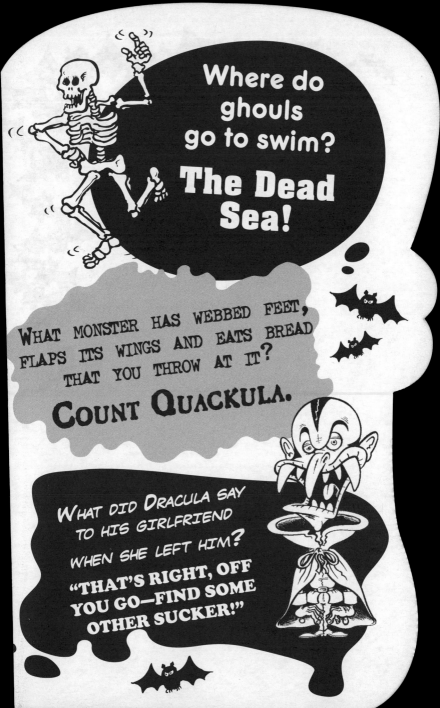

What do ghosts have in their cars?

Sheet belts!

WHAT'S THE SMARTEST THING TO DO IF A MONSTER COMES THROUGH YOUR FRONT DOOR?

Run out the back door!

WHY IS IT SAFE TO TELL A SKELETON A SECRET?

BECAUSE EVERYTHING YOU TELL THEM GOES IN ONE EAR AND OUT THE OTHER.

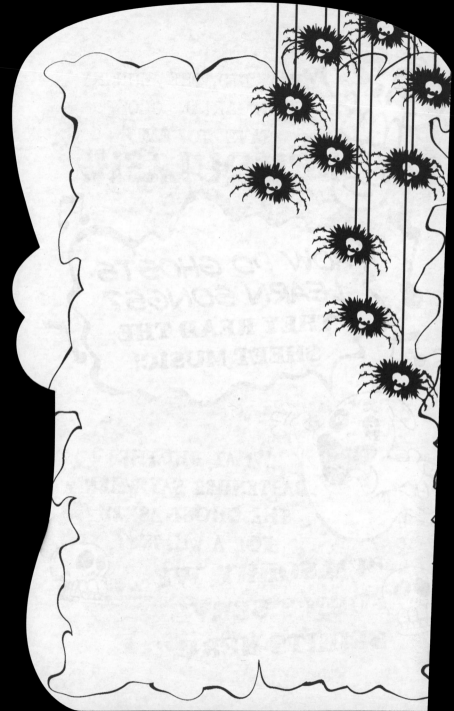

HOW DOES A GIRL VAMPIRE FLIRT?

SHE BATS HER EYES!

IF KING KONG WENT TO HONG KONG TO PLAY PING-PONG AND HAVE A SING-SONG AND THEN DIED, WHAT WOULD THEY PUT ON HIS COFFIN?

A LID!

WHERE IN THE WILD WEST WOULD YOU FIND A LOT OF GHOSTS?

TOMBSTONE.

FOR SALE

1910 HEARSE. VERY GOOD CONDITION. ORIGINAL BODY!

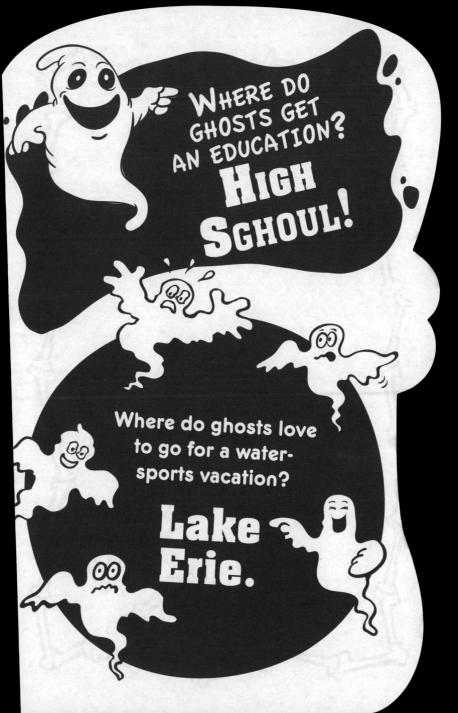

HOW DO GHOSTS LIKE THEIR SOFT DRINKS?

ICE GHOUL!

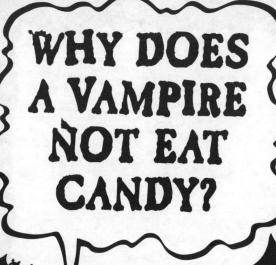

WHAT DO GOBLINS MAIL HOME WHILE ON VACATION?

GHOSTCARDS!

What is a ghoul's favorite drink?

DEMON-ADE.

Where did the ghouls go on their trip?

They went from ghost to ghost.

WHAT IS A GHOST'S FAVORITE DAY OF THE WEEK?

Fright-day! The day after Thirst-day!

WHAT DO YOU GET IF YOU CROSS A MUMMY WITH A VAMPIRE?

A BLOOD-SUCKING BANDAGE.

HOW DO GHOSTS LIKE THEIR EGGS COOKED?

TERRI-FRIED!

What did Mama ghost say to her son?

"Don't spook until you're spooken to!"

When is it bad luck to be followed by a black cat?

When you're a mouse !

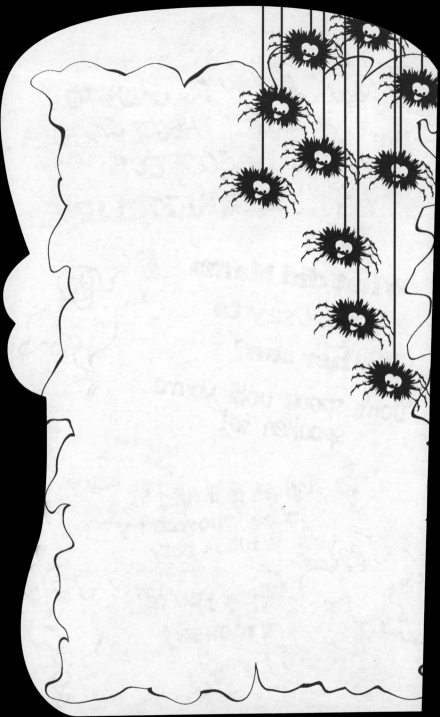

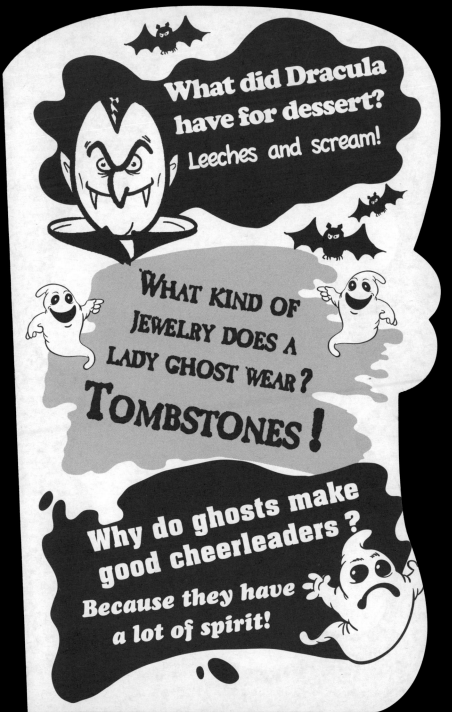

What does Dracula say when he is introduced?

"Hello, I'm very pleased to eat you!"

Why did Dracula have to go to jail?

Because he robbed the blood bank!

WHY DID THE VAMPIRE'S LUNCH DISAGREE WITH HIM?

HE ATE A STAKE SANDWICH.

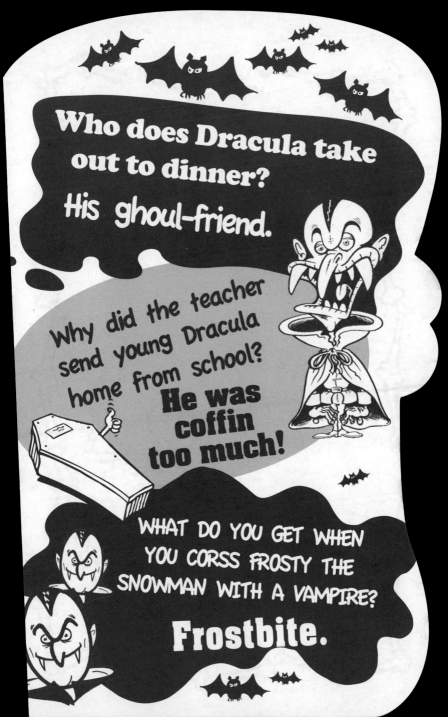

Why didn't Dracula ever get married?

He never met a nice enough ghoul!

Why do demons hang around with ghouls?

Because demons are a ghoul's best friend!

How do you make a milkshake?

Creep up behind a glass of milk and yell "Boo"!